WHAT'S BUGGING BUBBLES?

by Tracey West

Based on
"THE POWERPUFF GIRLS,"
as created by Craig McCracken

SCHOLASTIC INC.

New York   Toronto   London   Auckland   Sydney
Mexico City   New Delhi   Hong Kong

ISBN 0-439-25054-4

Designed by Peter Koblish
Illustrated by The Thompson Brothers

12 11 10 9 8 7 6 5 4 3 2   1 2 3 4 5 6/0

Printed in the U.S.A.

First Scholastic printing, February 2001

The city of Townsville!
Spring was here. Birds were singing. Flowers were blooming. . . .

Professor Utonium was working on his garden.

The Powerpuff Girls helped.

Blossom planted seeds.

Bubbles watered the pretty flowers.

Buttercup pulled weeds.

"What are you doing, Professor?" Bubbles asked.

"These slugs are eating everything in the garden," Professor Utonium said. He put salt on a little slug.

"What does the salt do?" asked Blossom.

"Salt makes slugs shrink," said the Professor.

"They get very small. Then *poof*! No more slug. Then the garden is safe."

"Cool!" said Buttercup.

"Oh, no!" cried Bubbles.

Bubbles felt sorry for the slug.
She did not want it to disappear.

"Do not worry, little guy," said Bubbles.
"I will not let the Professor shrink you."

Bubbles spotted the Professor's special growth juice.

That gave her an idea.

"This will make you big and strong," Bubbles told the slug.

The juice worked! The slug grew bigger. "Good-bye!" said Bubbles. "You will be safe now."

Bubbles did not tell her sisters about the slug.
She wanted it to be safe.
   Suddenly, the hot line rang!

"Let's go, Girls!" Blossom told her sisters.

Zip! Zoom! Zap! The Powerpuff Girls were off in a flash.

Chomp! Crunch! The slug was eating all the trees in Townsville.

Blossom and Buttercup flew into action.

Pow! "Take that!" cried Blossom.

Bam! "So long, Sluggo!" yelled Buttercup.

"It is all my fault," Bubbles said. "I made the slug big with the Professor's growth juice. Please do not hurt it."

"So what?" said Buttercup. "It is still just a slug. Let's smash it!"

"No!" Bubbles cried. "Let me talk to it."

Buttercup frowned. "You have one minute," she said. "If that slug does not stop, then we will bash it good!"

"Please stop eating all the trees!" Bubbles begged the slug.

But the slug kept chomping and chewing.

"I think it is hungry," Bubbles said.

"Oh, no!" Blossom shouted. "The slug is headed for the park! It will eat all the trees! It will slime all the people!"

Bubbles started to cry. "I did not want the slug to become a monster," she said. "I just did not want the Professor to put salt on it and make it shrink."

WNSVILLE'S OWN SALTY SN

That gave Blossom an idea. "Salt! We can use salt to shrink it!"

"But where are we going to get that much salt?" Buttercup asked.

The Girls did not need superpowers to find the salt. It was right under their noses! They took as much salt as they could. . . .

They put the salt on the slug.

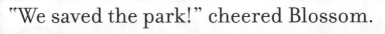

"We saved the park!" cheered Blossom.

"We saved the slug!" cheered Bubbles.

"I still want to smash something," Buttercup grumbled.

The Girls flew back to the garden.

So once again, the day is saved,
thanks to The Powerpuff Girls!